This igloo book belongs to:

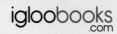

Published in 2012
by Igloo Books Ltd
Cottage Farm
Sywell
Northants
NN6 0BJ
www.igloobooks.com

REX001 0812
2 4 6 8 10 9 7 5 3 1
ISBN: 978-0-85780-686-4

Printed and manufactured in China

The Night Before
CHRISTMAS

igloobooks
.com

It was the night before Christmas and all through the house,
Nothing was stirring, not even a mouse.
The stockings were hung up with care,
In hopes that Santa Claus soon would be there.

The children were nestled, all snug in their beds,
While dreams of presents filled up their heads.

Then out on the lawn, there came a great clatter,
I sprang from my bed to see what was the matter.
I flew to the window, as quick as a flash,
tore open the shutters and threw up the sash.

The moon glittered over the fresh-fallen snow
and moonbeams shone on the garden below.
Then suddenly, what do you think should appear,
but a sparkling sleigh and eight reindeer!

They flew by in a flurry without ever a pause.
And sitting behind them was Santa Claus!
The reindeer flew round, at top speed they came,
Santa whistled and called each one by name.

"Go Dasher! Go Dancer! Go Prancer and Vixen!
Fly, Comet! Fly, Cupid! Fly Donner and Blitzen!
Over the garden and along by the wall.
Fly away reindeer, fly away all!"

As dry leaves in the wind, whirl up and fly,
Twisting and turning, drawn up to the sky.
So up to the house-top the reindeers they flew,
With the sleigh full of toys and Santa Claus, too.

Just then I heard a strange sound on the roof,
The prancing and pawing of each little hoof.
I listened a moment and then turned around,
As down the chimney Santa came with a bound.

He was dressed all in red from his head to his foot,
And his clothes showed smudges of dark chimney soot.
A bundle of toys he had flung on his back and he
Looked like a peddler, just opening his pack.

His kind brown eyes
Were twinkly and merry.
His cheeks were like roses,
His nose like a cherry!
He looked at the mince pies
and warm milky drink.
Then, he settled himself down
in a chair with a wink.

His mince pies all eaten, he opened his sack.
He took out some presents and put the other ones back.
Santa gave a chuckle and then tapped his nose,
The presents all sparkled with shimmering bows.

Santa filled up the stockings and tapped on his nose.
With a happy chuckle up to the chimney he rose.
Outside on the roof, Santa made his way back to
The jingling reindeer with his big present sack.

With a lightness of foot, Santa sprang to his sleigh.
He took up the reins and said, "Reindeer Away!"
Santa was happy, the night's work was nearly done.
"Ho-ho-ho!" he cried. "Merry Christmas, Everyone!"

"Goodbye, Merry Christmas!"

The Night Before CHRISTMAS

Illustrated by
Tom Sperling

Let this wonderful, timeless rhyme carry you off into an
enchanted world of soft falling snow and twinkling lights.
This festive classic contains all the mystery and magic of
Christmas Eve and the excitement of waiting for Santa to arrive.
Make this beautiful story part of your family tradition
and every Christmas will be a very merry one!

Also available:

UK   £9.99
US $19.95
CAN $19.95

CE

ISBN 978-0-85780-686-4

igloobooks
.com

9 780857 806864